Little Angel

Little Angel  a hand

"Why do you accept the tasks I ask you to do? Is it just for the pleasure of earning wings?"

The little angel gasped. "How can you ask that?"

"I just want you to think about why you do things."

"Well, I know the answer to this one for sure," said the little angel. "I do the tasks because I want to help children."

"Good," said the archangel. "Let's go help someone."

Titles in the

Angelwings

Pocket Books series

Angelwings

Give and Take

Donna Jo Napoli

illustrations by Lauren Klementz-Harte

POCKET
BOOKS

Thank you to all my family,
Brenda Bowen, Nöelle Paffett-Lugassy and Richard Tchen

POCKET
BOOKS

An imprint of Simon & Schuster UK Ltd
Africa House, 64 - 78 Kingsway, London WC2B 6AH

Text © copyright 2000 by Donna Jo Napoli
Illustrations © copyright 2000 by Lauren Klementz-Harte
Cover design by Blacksheep © Simon & Schuster

Designed by Steve Scott
The text for this book was set in
Minister Light and Cheltenham.
The illustrations were rendered in ink and wash.

A CIP catalogue record for this book is available
from the British Library

ISBN 0 7434 0838 1

1 3 5 7 9 10 8 6 4 2

Printed by Omnia Books Ltd, Glasgow

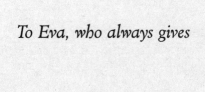

To Eva, who always gives

Angelwings

Give and Take

Angel Talk

he Little Angel of Generosity smoothed the sheet of wrapping paper flat. Then he carefully rolled the yo-yo up into the paper. He didn't have ribbon, but the white twine did just fine. He tied a firm knot and stayed squatting, with his arms crossed at his chest, viewing his handiwork. A pile of five presents for his four best friends, plus one extra—for himself. After all, he loved yo-yos, too.

"Are they for a party?" asked the Archangel of Generosity.

"Oh, I didn't see you there." The little angel jumped to his feet. "No, they're just for fun."

The archangel smiled and picked up the spool of twine. She played with the loose end. "Only five. Are these for little angels?"

1

"Yes. Including me." The little angel gave a small yank on the archangel's sleeve. "Why are you here? Have you got a task for me?"

The Archangel of Generosity lined up the presents in a neat row. "Nothing for the archangels?"

"Archangels don't need anything."

The archangel put her hands on her hips. "Who says?"

The little angel laughed. "Come on. You can have anything you want, anytime you want it."

"Can I have one of these presents?"

"No," yelped the little angel. "I only have five."

"Well, then, I can't have anything I want after all, can I?"

The Little Angel of Generosity screwed up his mouth. "What's your point?"

"Think about it."

"You wouldn't even like what's in the wrapping paper," said the little angel. "It's for kids. Plus, it's not a girl thing anyway."

"How do you know?" asked the archangel. "Think about that, too. But in the meantime, you're right: I do have a task for you."

"Great." The little angel grinned wide. "All I need is one more task, and a bell will ring because I'll have enough feathers to earn my wings."

The Archangel of Generosity rubbed the back of her neck in thought. "Why do you accept the tasks I ask you to do? Is it just for the pleasure of earning wings?"

The little angel gasped. "How can you ask that?"

"I just want you to think about why you do things."

"Well, I know the answer to this one for sure," said the little angel. "I do the tasks because I want to help children."

"So you don't care about your wings?"

"Yes, I care. I want my wings a lot. I can't wait to hear the bell that will ring when I earn them. I'll fly everywhere. But that's just a nice extra. A wonderful extra. The real point is to help children."

"Good," said the archangel. "Let's go help someone."

Art

"I already know what I'm getting." Setha clasped her hands behind her back and rocked from foot to foot.

"You look like a penguin," said Dinah quietly.

Setha kept rocking, her hands still behind her back. "It's so terrific. Mommy bought all these art materials. I'm getting a five-pound box of clay. I can make pinch pots and coil bowls and anything I want."

Dinah kicked the toe of her sneaker into the dirt. "If you dig in the right spots, you can find clay. You don't have to buy it."

"Not like this clay. It's self-hardening. I don't even need a kiln."

Dinah dug deeper with her sneaker. "The ground is hard here. I think there's clay right beneath our feet."

"Gray clay, yuck. The clay Mommy bought me is red-brown. It's from Mexico and it's so beautiful, Dinah, you wouldn't believe it." Setha swayed her head from side to side as though she were listening to private music inside her head. Her braid swung in a wide arc. "And Mommy even got me the acrylic paints I wanted. They go perfect on clay. I can decorate whatever I make."

"Why buy colored clay if you're only going to paint it other colors?"

"I won't paint every inch. Just patterns. And acrylics are the best. They're so bright, they look like plastic. The set has eight colors. Eight."

Dinah looked from her best friend to the ground. Red-brown clay that hardened all by itself was something wonderful. "How much did it cost?"

"The set of acrylics?"

"No, the clay."

"I don't know. Mommy bought me water-

7

color paints, too. And the right kind of paper for them. And these great brushes that hold a fine point when you get the tip wet. I don't know how much any of it costs and I don't care. It's for my birthday."

Dinah smiled. "You're a good artist."

"I'm not so good yet. But I'm going to be." Setha caught her long braid, pulled it forward over her shoulder, and played with the tips of it. "You need new sneakers."

Dinah looked down. The sole of her right shoe was separating from the top at the toe end. "Maybe I'll ask my dad for sneakers for my birthday. But that's not for a few months yet."

"I know. So . . . ?" Setha's voice rose in a question.

"So what?"

Setha laughed. "So what are you getting me for mine? Mine is next week."

Dinah blinked. "I can't tell you. You need at least one surprise."

"I'll get plenty of surprises. Daddy always surprises me. And so does Lil."

Lil was Setha's big sister. She was usually pretty nice to Setha. Dinah liked her. Lil was bound to get Setha something really nice.

Dinah had no idea what she'd get Setha— or where she'd find the money to get Setha anything she'd really like. "Well, I'll surprise you, too."

Angel Talk

"Is Setha's family rich?" asked the Little Angel of Generosity.

"Not rich, no. But they do okay." The archangel smiled mischievously. "You'd probably say they can have anything they want. But I wouldn't say that."

The little angel flushed. "Do you still want one of those little presents I wrapped?"

"Little presents, huh? Are you trying to make them sound insignificant? Presents are presents. And I love presents."

"But if I give you one, I don't get one," said the little angel.

"Hmm. That's often the way it is with gifts. That's part of the gift."

The Little Angel of Generosity picked at his elbow. "I think I'm getting a wart."

"Put banana peel on it," said the archangel.

"Really? Does that work?"

"Try it and see." The archangel smiled. "Tape a piece of banana peel to it for a few days."

"Okay." The little angel smiled back. "Anyway, I've already got some good ideas about how to help Setha be more generous."

"Setha?" The Archangel of Generosity laughed. "Setha? She's not your assignment."

"She isn't?"

"Not at all."

"But Setha was talking about the presents she's going to get for her birthday. And Dinah doesn't even have decent shoes. Dinah's poor, isn't she?"

"I suppose you could call her poor."

"So Setha has to be generous to her," said the little angel.

"Setha knows perfectly well how to be generous. It's Dinah who needs help."

"Dinah doesn't have nearly as much as

Setha. You heard the way she was talking. If she wanted clay, she'd have to dig it out of the ground. How could Dinah need to learn how to be generous?"

"Think about it, little angel. Just watch and think."

Money

Nathaniel climbed onto Dinah's tummy and sat there. He waited a moment, then he bounced on his butt. "Wake up, Dinah. Wake up."

Dinah was already awake. She'd held her eyes almost closed and watched Nathaniel through her eyelashes standing beside her bed and finally losing patience and climbing onto her. She knew it was late morning, but somehow she didn't want to get out of bed.

"Get dressed. Daddy's going to have the oil changed on the car. And you're supposed to take me and Eric to Riverside Park."

"Why can't Jason do it?"

"He's got a baseball game. That's why we're going to Riverside—to watch him."

"Jason's always got a baseball game."

o, he doesn't." Nathaniel lay forward and put his fat little cheek on Dinah's.

Dinah opened her eyes. It didn't matter, anyway; Nathaniel knew she was awake because she had answered him. She sighed and folded her arms around Nathaniel. He snuggled against her. Poor Nathaniel. He missed having a mother more than any of the rest of them, and he couldn't even remember their mother. She'd left before he'd learned to walk.

Four years ago.

Dinah remembered her. But less and less all the time. "I don't want to go to Riverside today. I don't want to watch Jason play ball."

Nathaniel sat up. "Are you sick?"

"No. I have to go shopping."

"Okay." Nathaniel climbed off happily.

Okay? Just like that? "You aren't going to whine?"

"No. Daddy said if you won't do it, me and Eric have to go to the garage with him."

14

Nathaniel grinned. "I love the garage. I love the black shiny oil. I'll go tell Daddy." He raced out of the room before Dinah had had a proper chance to think about that.

Well, it wasn't her fault if Daddy had to have Eric and Nathaniel underfoot all day. Dinah was going to spend her day buying Setha a birthday present, and that's all there was to it.

Dinah stretched, got dressed, brushed her teeth, and went into the kitchen.

Daddy stood at the counter in front of the electric waffle iron. "Good morning, sleepy-head."

Jason and Eric sat at the table gobbling waffles. Eric smiled at Dinah, but Jason didn't even look up. Nathaniel galloped around the table.

"I hear you're going shopping." Daddy opened the waffle iron and put two hot ones on a plate. He held it out to Dinah. "What do you need?"

Dinah took the plate and sat down. She needed sneakers, for one. What would Daddy say if Dinah told him she wanted new sneakers? "I have to buy a birthday present for Setha."

"You can't go to the mall alone," said Jason, his mouth full. "She can't, can she, Dad?"

"I'm not going to the mall. I'm going to the art store next door to the library." It was an easy walk, and Dinah had been allowed to go there alone for the past couple of years.

"It's chilly this morning. I'll drop you off." Daddy picked up his mug of coffee and went into the living room. "There's a box of clothes here for you to look through, Dinah," he called over his shoulder.

Clothes? Dinah stuffed a big bite of waffle in her mouth and ran into the living room. A cardboard box sat on the couch. On the very top was a pair of neatly folded jeans. Dinah held them up. They smelled of detergent.

Underneath was a brown sweater with yellow flowers embroidered on it. All of it was used. "Where did this stuff come from?"

Daddy took his jacket off the hook. "Charlene's new neighbor has a girl just a couple of years older than you."

Charlene was their housekeeper. She was there Monday through Friday, all day long. Somehow she was always coming up with clothes for Dinah. Daddy bought new clothes for Jason. He said it was worth it because after Jason, Eric could use them, and then Nathaniel could ruin whatever Eric hadn't destroyed. But no one else could wear Dinah's clothes, so it didn't make sense to buy her new things.

Grandma used to buy Dinah something new at Christmas and on her birthday. In fact, one year Grandma had bought Dinah a velvet nightgown. It was ruby colored, and Dinah had felt like a princess when she'd worn it. She still had that nightgown—folded in her bottom drawer—even though she'd out-grown it long ago. But these days Grandma gave her money because she said Dinah was old enough to choose things for herself.

Dinah searched through the box of old clothes. Yes, there were shoes, too. Sneakers. They were navy blue and suede and ugly. But they were in good condition, and Dinah could tell they would fit her with enough room to grow—as Daddy liked to say. Just once, Dinah would like to go to the store and pick whatever sneakers she wanted, without thinking about the price. But Grandma never gave enough for something as expensive as sneakers.

"How much do you need?" Daddy took out his wallet.

Dinah jumped. She flushed with instant guilt. "What?"

"For Setha's present."

Oh, that's all. Dinah swallowed in relief. "I still have money left from what Grandma sent at Christmas."

Daddy nodded and quickly put his wallet away.

Dinah ran into the bedroom she shared with Nathaniel and opened the envelope she kept her money in. Sixteen dollars. That was a lot. She could get Setha a great present for sixteen dollars. But then she'd have nothing left. She plucked out a five-dollar bill, stuffed it in her jeans pocket, put the rest of the money back in the envelope, and tried to shut the drawer. But it wouldn't shut. She pushed hard. The drawer was stuck.

Dinah looked at the envelope. Everything in that art store cost a lot. She knew because she and Setha had stood outside many times and read the price labels on the things in the display window. Maybe she should take all the money, after all. She grabbed the envelope and pushed on the drawer again. This time it shut with a *bang*.

Angel Talk

"Did you do something to make that drawer not close?" The Archangel of Generosity looked firmly at the little angel, but her eyes were smiling, weren't they?

"That's what you wanted me to do," said the little angel. "This way, Dinah can get a good gift for Setha."

"But she could have gotten a gift for five dollars."

"Sure," said the little angel. "But if she spends all her money, then she can get a better gift. That's what you said before, remember? Sometimes giving presents means not having something for yourself."

"Oh, little angel, I didn't mean that you should have to suffer every time you give a present. I just meant that the joy of giving should come first. True generosity is giving from your heart."

"Oh," said the little angel. "Oh, no. Now Dinah's going to spend every penny she has on Setha, when she didn't have to."

"Don't worry about it," said the archangel. "She's not so poor that she's going to starve without that money."

"But she would rather spend it on something for herself."

"Probably." The archangel nodded.

"So now she'll resent giving whatever she buys to Setha."

"Hmmm," said the archangel, rubbing the back of her neck. "You might have just made your job a little harder, because it's up to you to make sure that doesn't happen."

Tools

The art store was small, with shelves that went from the floor all the way to the ceiling. Dinah walked slowly down each aisle, looking carefully. She stopped in front of the clay.

"Can I help you?" The clerk came up beside Dinah.

"I'm looking for a gift."

"For a friend? Someone your age?"

"Yes. She's an artist."

The clerk smiled. "How much were you thinking of spending?"

"I don't know. I just want something nice."

"Does she paint? We have some vivid temperas that came in last week." The clerk pointed to the next set of shelves. "Why don't you take a look? If anything's too high, call me over and I'll get it down for you." She went

back to the front checkout counter.

Dinah turned around and faced the clay. The cheapest self-drying kind was gray and from Italy. Only six dollars. It weighed two pounds and it was soft to the touch. Dinah could squish her thumb in even through the plastic wrapping. The next cheapest was gray clay from America. Eight dollars. It weighed five pounds, so, actually, it was a lot cheaper per pound than the Italian clay. It was harder, too. Dinah didn't know if that meant it was better or worse. Probably worse, since it cost less per pound. And there was the Mexican clay—in a rusty-colored box. If the clay was the color of the box, it was perfect for Setha's room, which was a pale yellow. Twelve dollars.

Dinah had sixteen dollars. She could buy the Mexican clay if she wanted. But that would be stupid, anyway, because Setha was already getting that clay from her mother.

Beautiful clay.

Dinah pulled her jacket tight around her chest and stared at the box.

Dinah shared a room with Nathaniel, and Jason shared a room with Eric. But Daddy said that when Dinah was big enough, Nathaniel would move in with the boys, because a girl needed her own room after a while. The room was white now, but when it belonged to Dinah, she'd be able to paint it any color she wanted. She could paint it pale yellow, too. Then anything made out of that Mexican clay would look perfect in her room.

On the shelf below the clay were stacked wooden boxes of various sizes. Dinah opened the top one. It held a row of little tools. They had thin wood handles with blades at the end. Some of the blades were scooped, like shallow spoons; some were wide; all were sharp. Dinah knew immediately that they were for working with the clay. Setha could dig out lovely designs on the sides of the things that she made. A bowl with bunnies all around. Or a box for barrettes, with mer-maids on the top. That's what Dinah would make if she had clay and those tools.

She closed the box and turned it upside down. Twenty dollars. Twenty dollars for just this small box of six tools. The other boxes were bigger; they were sure to cost more. Dinah put the box back on the stack.

She took her envelope of money out of her jacket pocket.

She looked over her shoulder at the front counter.

The clerk was on the phone.

Dinah's hand shot out, and with one swift move, the toolbox was tucked under her left arm, inside her jacket—where no one could see it. Her body went rigid; her head felt light. She walked up the aisle.

She couldn't open the front door. Her hand was too clumsy, what with the money enve-lope still in it. She held the envelope between her teeth and pulled on the door. Then she pushed. The door wouldn't budge. She felt sick.

"Didn't you find anything you want?" The clerk put down the phone. "I can help you look."

Dinah turned around, holding her arm to her side so hard that the edges of the toolbox dug into her armpit.

"I saw you looking at the clay. Didn't you like any of it?"

Dinah took the envelope out from between her teeth. "I like the Mexican clay," she managed to say.

"Oh, yes. That's fine quality. A very good gift. Shall I get it for you?" The clerk walked to the clay shelf as she talked. She came back to the counter with a box of clay. "That will be twelve dollars and seventy-two cents altogether. Is that all right?"

Dinah nodded. She looked at the money envelope in her hand. She didn't dare move her left arm, and she couldn't get the money out of the envelope with just her right hand, so she gave the whole envelope to the clerk.

The clerk opened the envelope gingerly, being careful not to touch the teeth marks. "There's only eleven dollars in here." She blinked several times.

Dinah felt hot all over. How stupid of her. The other five dollars was still in her jeans pocket. Dinah reached under her jacket and dug into her pocket. She prayed that the bottom of the toolbox didn't show. She handed the bill to the clerk.

The clerk smiled in obvious relief. "Well, now, here's your change. I hope your friend likes the clay."

Dinah took the change and the bag with the clay, and left.

Angel Talk

"Dinah's a thief." The Little Angel of Generosity dropped his face in his hands.

The archangel patted his back.

"This is terrible," mumbled the little angel.

"Yes."

The little angel looked up at the archangel. "I kept her from leaving the store when she first tried to go. I thought that if she couldn't open the door, she'd have a moment to realize what she'd done and she'd turn around and put the toolbox back. But then that clerk got the clay off the shelf, and everything went wrong."

"I know," said the archangel.

"And then I didn't have the heart to hold the door shut again. The clerk was looking and

30

she would have wondered what was wrong and Dinah would have gotten caught."

"I know," said the archangel.

"Oh, I did bad," said the little angel. "I shouldn't have let her get away with it. I didn't know what to do and I did everything wrong."

"It's not your fault. You can't control Dinah's actions. All you can do is try to help guide her."

"But you wouldn't have let her get out of the store with that box hidden under her jacket, would you?"

"I couldn't have stopped her," said the archangel. "Dinah made a choice. It was the wrong choice, and she knew it. But sometimes we have to make mistakes in order to figure out how we want to live."

"I don't understand anything," said the little angel. "I'm supposed to help Dinah be generous, not honest. This isn't the right task for me."

"Oh, I think it is. Just keep watching. You'll find ways to help her."

Eric

Dinah got home before everyone else. She ran into her bedroom, closed the door, and dropped the heavy bag with the clay onto her bed. Then she took the box of tools out from under her jacket and set it on the bed, too.

The box looked small and harmless. Dinah opened it. The tools were all still there. She sat on the bed and picked them up, one by one, imagining how to use them.

The clerk in the art store had been nice. If she knew Dinah had stolen this box of tools, she'd hate her.

Dinah had never stolen anything before. Her heart was still beating hard.

If Dinah gave Setha the box of tools and Setha found out they were stolen, she'd hate Dinah, too.

But Setha would never find out unless Dinah told her. Still, it felt bad to give a stolen present.

Maybe Dinah should just keep both the clay and the tools. Setha was going to get lots of fabulous presents, anyway. She didn't need these tools. And Dinah had never had anything that fabulous in her life.

Dinah opened the box of clay. Inside, a plastic bag kept the clay from drying out. Dinah opened the little twisty on the plastic bag. The clay smelled earthy and clean.

Too clean for a thief.

"What's that?" came Eric's voice. He stood in the doorway.

"You didn't knock." Dinah closed the plastic bag and shut the box.

"The door was open."

"No, it wasn't. I closed it."

"Well, then, it opened itself." Eric came over and stood by the bed. "You bought Setha two gifts. Wow."

"The clay's for me." Dinah pressed her lips together. Then she added quickly, "I paid twelve dollars and seventy-two cents for it."

"That's a lot," said Eric. He was in third grade and he knew a little bit about money these days. He liked to talk about how much comic books cost and who had gotten the better deal in trading them at school. He picked up the toolbox and opened it. "These are great."

"Be careful. They're sharp."

Eric closed the box. "You'd better wrap them up so Nathaniel doesn't touch them." He turned the box over. "Twenty dollars. Wow. Where did you get twenty dollars from?"

Dinah looked Eric hard in the face. In some ways, he was her favorite brother. He didn't ask her to be his mother, like Nathaniel did. And he didn't act like she was a little kid, like Jason did. She couldn't remember ever having lied to him. "I didn't. I stole the box."

"You stole it!" Eric's mouth stayed open. His eyes filled with tears. "You always told me never to steal anything. But look what you did."

Dinah tried to keep her face calm. "I didn't mean to. It just sort of happened."

Eric shook his head. "How can you steal something without meaning to?"

"Setha will love it, and I couldn't afford it and—"

"Then you should have gotten her something you could afford."

Dinah felt her face crumple. "You're right."

"And you shouldn't have bought yourself clay."

Dinah hadn't intended to buy the clay. She only did it to keep the clerk from being suspicious of her. But there was no point in fighting Eric over it. He was right. And he didn't even know she'd been thinking about keeping the toolbox. If he knew, he'd be that much more disgusted with her. How did he get to be so grown up so fast? "You're right," she whispered.

37

"So what are you going to do now?" Eric handed the box back to Dinah.

"Are you going to tell Daddy on me?"

"You know I wouldn't do that." Eric sat on the bed beside Dinah.

"Do you hate me, Eric?"

"I love you. But you shouldn't steal. What are you going to do now?"

Angel Talk

Were you part of getting Dinah to tell Eric the truth?" asked the archangel.

The Little Angel of Generosity shook his head. "All I did was open the bedroom door. I was hoping her father would catch her."

"Thank heavens for Eric," said the archangel. "He's younger than Dinah, but he's got a lot of sense."

"No, he doesn't. If he wants Dinah to get out of this mess, he should tell his father."

"Dinah has to want to get out of this mess first."

The Little Angel of Generosity threw up his hands. "She does want to get out of this mess. You heard: She asked Eric if he hated her. She's miserable."

"But not for the right reason," said the archangel.

"What's the right reason?" asked the little angel.

"Think about it. And remember: I chose you for this task, not any other little angel."

TV

Jason washed the last dish and put it in the dish drainer. "Time for TV."

Dinah dried the dish and handed it to Eric.

"Yay!" Eric put it away.

Nathaniel stopped wiping off the chairs and threw his dishcloth in the sink. "I love TV."

They filed into the living room. Saturday night TV was a tradition. Daddy didn't allow TV on school nights unless they had already finished their homework. But usually by the time Jason finished all his work, it was bedtime, anyway. And Friday night they always did something special—like go bowling or rent a video. But Saturday was always TV night.

Dinah looked forward to it because it felt cozy. Tonight she needed to feel cozy. "Aren't you coming, Daddy?"

Daddy sat at the little desk near the hallway. "I have to finish balancing the checkbook first."

Jason picked up the remote control and flipped through the channels.

Two little kids stood on a sidewalk hugging each other with people running all around them and a fire engine in the street.

Jason flipped on.

But a moment later the scene was back. The TV newsman was telling about a terrible fire.

"What's the matter with this remote control?" Jason flipped past that channel.

But again the scene came back. And now Dinah could see the two kids off to the side behind the TV newsman. The little boy was crying.

"This thing is broken." Jason dropped the remote control on the couch and sat in front of the TV, working the channel buttons at the bottom.

"Hey, go back to the fire," said Dinah.

"Who wants to watch news?" Jason punched another button. "Oh, there's a good movie on here."

"I want to see the news first," said Dinah.

"No one wants the news," said Jason. He went back and sat on the couch.

Nathaniel climbed on his lap. "I love movies," he said.

Eric looked at Dinah and shrugged apologetically. He sat beside Jason and Nathaniel.

Dinah walked over to Daddy and stood behind his chair.

Daddy subtracted a few more figures. Then he closed the checkbook and put it in the drawer. He looked at Dinah. "What's this about a fire on the news?"

"A house burned down."

"I hope no one got killed."

"The newsman said no one even got hurt."

"Well, that's a blessing."

"But they lost everything they had," said

44

Dinah. "There were two kids and they stood outside and watched everything they had burn."

Daddy made a little click with his tongue. "As long as the family wasn't hurt, that's all that matters."

"No, it's not. People care about things, Daddy. I mean, I know that other people matter more than things, but things matter, too. You just don't understand."

Daddy took Dinah's hand. "What don't I understand, Dinah?"

Dinah hadn't cried when the clerk stopped her at the door of the art store. And she hadn't cried when Eric looked at her so shocked in the bedroom. But now, all of a sudden, she had to fight back tears. "Those kids had things they loved. Everybody has things they love. Or they want to have things they love. If they can afford them."

Daddy stood up and led Dinah by the hand into the kitchen. They sat down beside each other, and Daddy kept holding her hand. "What are you talking about? What's bothering you?"

"I know having a housekeeper is expensive. And I know you don't make a lot of money. And I know four children cost a lot to feed. And I know all that." Dinah couldn't stop the tears now. "I know all that."

"So what is it you don't know, Dinah?"

"I want things, Daddy. Just like everyone else."

"What sort of things do you want?"

"Well, everything. New sneakers. And art materials. And everything."

"That's not just like everyone else." Daddy put Dinah's hands together and rubbed them between his own. "Not everyone has new sneakers and art materials. Lots of people don't have as much as you have, Dinah."

Dinah nodded. "I know that, too," she said. "But I can't help wanting things. Plus I need to buy Setha a birthday present."

"I thought you already did that, with your Christmas money from Grandma."

"I spent it on something for me," said Dinah, which was true. She had decided to keep both the toolbox and the clay for herself.

"Well, I can give you ten dollars for a present for Setha," said Daddy. "But as for the rest of it, you've got some figuring to do."

"What do you mean?"

"You want things. How are you going to get them? I'm having trouble making ends meet as it is, Dinah. So the answer can't come from me. What do you plan to do?"

Dinah sat up taller. Daddy sounded just like Eric. That was funny, when she came to think of it. She wiped her cheeks. "Maybe I could earn money."

"Doing what?"

"Well, I'm good at cleaning. I could ask neighbors if they need my help."

"That's a good idea."

Dinah thought about the Ferralls, down

the street. They had two little kids, and the mother always seemed to be about to lose her mind. She'd be a good one to ask. And then there was the old couple, right across the street: the Chens. They probably had a hundred chores they could use help with. And there were other people, too.

"Is there anything else you want to talk about?" asked Daddy.

Dinah looked at her father. He worked hard and he was a good daddy. He didn't need extra problems. Besides, she had no idea what he'd do if she told him she'd stolen something. No one in the family had ever done anything so bad. She shook her head.

Angel Talk

I think I need lessons in patience." The Little Angel of Generosity tapped his foot. "Dinah had the perfect opportunity to tell her father everything and she didn't."

"Keep working on her," said the archangel.

"I don't know what to do next. I pushed the TV channel back to that fire over and over so that she'd understand that some people have less than her family does. And her father even said that in so many words. But Dinah doesn't understand."

The archangel smiled. "So you're the reason the remote control didn't work. That was clever of you."

"But ineffective. All she thought about was how nice it would be to have things she loves."

"Just like you think about how nice it will be

49

to open your little pile of presents with your friends?"

"That's not fair," said the little angel. "I love what's in those presents. But you wouldn't even like it. It's not the same thing as with Dinah. I saw her put the box of tools in her drawer. So I bet she's planning on keeping it for herself."

"Don't you think she loves those tools?"

"Well, yes. But . . . " The little angel rubbed the back of his neck. "I'm confused now."

"You look like me when you rub the back of your neck." The archangel laughed. "Listen, little angel, I suspect Dinah is confused, too. It's hard to think about the happiness of others if you feel sorry for yourself."

"I don't feel sorry for myself," said the little angel.

"You're right, then," said the archangel, "it's not the same thing as with Dinah. So for now, concentrate on her."

Work

Dinah rang Susan's bell. She had tried the Ferralls first, but no one was home. Then she'd tried the Chens. Again, no luck. She had been about to cross the street and go back home when she heard a *bang* on the porch next door to the Chens. That was Susan's house. Susan was old, but she liked all the kids to call her by her first name, anyway. She lived alone, and Dinah was pretty sure she didn't have a lot of extra money. But that noise from her porch was sort of like a beckoning. So Dinah went over.

Only Susan wasn't on the porch. Maybe she wasn't even home, either. She was sure taking a long time to answer.

Finally, the door opened. "Why, hello, Dinah. What a nice surprise." Susan was dressed in jeans and an old sweater. She brushed off her hands as though they were dirty.

"Hello, Susan. I'm trying to earn money. And I was hoping that maybe you'd have a job for me. I can clean anything—floors, bathrooms, windows. I could clean out your refrigerator for you."

Susan beamed. "You came just at the right time." She stepped back so Dinah could enter and she closed the door behind her. "I'm going through my attic, looking for things for that poor family."

"What poor family?"

"The one whose house burned down last night. They live right in Philadelphia. Didn't you see the news?"

"Yes, I did."

"Well, then, you know. They have nothing now. So I expect I can find something in that attic they could use. I've been storing boxes for the past thirty years." Susan led the way up the stairs. "It's awful dusty in there. Do you have allergies?"

"No," said Dinah. "I'm fine."

Susan lifted the hatch door, and Dinah peeked in. The attic was dark. And it smelled stale.

"There's a light with a pull switch somewhere near the center of the room if you can make your way over there," said Susan.

Dinah skirted around boxes and over piles of things until a cord hit her in the face. She pulled, and the bare bulb lit up the attic. There were stacks of books and record albums and picture frames scattered among boxes of all sizes.

"The clothes boxes could be anywhere. I didn't label things because I figured I'd never go through them again." Susan came the rest of the way up into the attic, staying bent so she wouldn't hit her head on the beams. "I guess that means I should have thrown them out."

"If you'd thrown them out, you wouldn't be able to give them away now," said Dinah.

Susan smiled. "I like the way you think."

So Dinah and Susan opened box after box. And every time a box had clothes in it, Dinah carried it down to Susan's living room. When they had checked every box, they shut off the light and went downstairs.

"Well, now, Dinah, that was good work. You can carry all these boxes, one by one, of course, to the library. They're collecting donations there."

"But don't you want to go through them first?"

"Why?"

"Well, there might be things you paid a lot of money for. A fancy dress or something."

Susan smiled. "I never had a lot of money. But if there is something nice in here that I can't remember, wouldn't that be wonderful? Can you imagine the pleasure they'd get from receiving not just useful things but useless things, too? Like in that book *A Child's Christmas in Wales*."

"I don't know that book."

"You don't? Well, it's wonderful. You should check it out from the library sometime." Susan picked her purse off the little side table with the lamp. "Here's five dollars for your help."

"Oh, that's way too much."

"Wait'll you've carried the boxes to the library. You won't think it's too much then." Susan opened the front door. "Put them all on my porch and just take them at your own pace. I think I'm going to nap awhile now. Thank you so much, Dinah."

Angel Talk

ive dollars already," said the little angel, jumping in place in excitement.

"Yes, Susan's generous." The archangel nodded, but she didn't look happy. "It was a stroke of luck for Dinah that she went to Susan's door."

"Not luck, actually." The Little Angel of Generosity cleared his throat and pulled himself up tall. "I made her go there."

"How?"

"I opened Susan's storm door and banged it shut so Dinah would look over at her porch."

"Oh, I wondered what made that noise. But how did you know Susan would need Dinah?"

"Well, I really wanted Dinah to earn money—"

"I can see that. Little angel, I think you're

getting sidetracked. Helping Dinah earn money isn't the goal here."

"I have a reason I want her to earn money. You'll see. Anyway, I visited all the neighbors, looking for someone who could use Dinah's help. And Susan turned out to be perfect because she was doing exactly the right kind of chore to make Dinah think."

"But did she make Dinah think?" The archangel rubbed the back of her neck. "I haven't heard Dinah say anything or seen her do anything that shows you're making any progress with her at all."

"Well, now, it's my turn to tell you to keep watching," said the little angel. "I've got a plan."

Boxes

Dinah carried box after box to the library. Since she could carry only one at a time, and since the library was a ten-minute walk away, it took her almost two hours to carry all of them. Susan was right: Five dollars didn't seem like that much, after all.

The man in charge of organizing the donations stacked Susan's boxes on the left side, every one of them, even though there were lots more boxes on the left side than on the right.

Dinah handed him the last box and turned to leave when she heard a crash. The box on the top of the left side had fallen off.

The man put it back.

"Why don't you put some of those boxes on the other side?" asked Dinah. "That way they won't fall."

"This side is for kitchen stuff and towels and sheets and big clothes. Things for adults. The other side is for kids' things."

Dinah leaned over and looked into an open box on the kids' side. It held baby clothes. Hadn't the donor watched the news? Those two kids in the fire couldn't wear baby clothes. The boy was older than Nathaniel. And the girl was probably as old as Eric. Maybe nothing in any of these boxes was right for the kids in the fire.

"Now how did this come open?" The man closed the top flaps of the box.

Dinah put her hands in her pockets and walked home. She fingered the five-dollar bill as she went.

Susan gave all those boxes to people she didn't even know. And Susan wasn't rich. But, then, it didn't cost anything for Susan to give away those things—she didn't want them, anyway.

Still, somehow Dinah felt sure that if Susan

hadn't had all those boxes stored up, she would have gone through her closets and picked out other clothes.

That was the right thing to do.

Susan would never steal anything. Eric would never steal anything.

And now Dinah was running. She burst into her house and ran to her bedroom.

Nathaniel sat on the floor surrounded by wooden blocks. "Come see, Dinah. I made a cave for my dinosaurs."

"That's nice, Nathaniel," Dinah said without looking. She opened her bottom drawer. There was the ruby-colored nightgown Grandma had given her. She rubbed it against her cheek. It was still as soft as ever. Dinah clutched it to her chest and dashed out of the room with Nathaniel at her heels. "Eric," she called. "Oh, Eric, there you are."

Eric and Jason were playing a video game in the living room. "What do you want?" asked Eric.

Dinah looked at her brothers, all three of them. "Daddy," she called.

Daddy came in from the kitchen. He had flour all down the front of his T-shirt. Daddy liked to experiment with baking on Sundays.

"Okay, everyone. We're going to make a box of things for the children whose house got burned down."

Jason looked up. "Who says?"

"I do. They're collecting donations at the library. But so far, most of the stuff is for adults. We're going to give kids' stuff."

"Will they take food?" asked Daddy. "I'm just about to bake three dozen cookies. We could give two dozen to them."

"If we put them in a tightly closed tin, I don't see how they could say no."

"I can give my Rubik's Cube," said Nathaniel, "the one we all got for prizes at Aunt Julie's wedding. I'm too little to do it right yet, anyway."

"You'll grow, stupid," said Jason.

"Oh. I'll keep my Rubik's Cube."

"No," said Dinah. "Give me yours, Nathaniel. I never use mine. So when you're old enough, I'll give you mine."

"Are you giving that nightgown?" asked Eric.

"Yes."

"But you love it," said Eric.

"The little girl in the fire will love it, too."

"I have some extra comic books," said Eric. He went into his room and came back with two.

Jason stood up and stretched. Then he went into his room. He came back with a baseball. Dinah recognized it as the new one he'd gotten for Christmas. He handed it to Dinah without a word.

"I'm not giving my Rubik's Cube," said Nathaniel.

"Everyone should give something," said Dinah.

"I know. But everyone's giving something

63

they love, and I don't love my Rubik's Cube."
Nathaniel ran into his bedroom. He came
back with his teddy bear. "Here. I don't love
him as much as I love my rabbit, but I love
him."

Angel Talk

Well, you've got the whole family being generous." The Archangel of Generosity tapped the little angel's shoulder. "Fine job."

"How do you know I had anything to do with it?"

"You knocked the top box off the stack of adults' things. And you opened the box with the baby clothes just so Dinah could see." The archangel smiled. "I've come to recognize your work."

"I'm not done yet," said the little angel. "Tomorrow's going to be an important day."

"Good," said the archangel. "I'm looking forward to your next move. In the meantime, I think I'm going to sneak in Nathaniel and Dinah's room and play with a Rubik's Cube.

They won't even notice if one is missing for a while."

"Really? Do you like that sort of thing?"

"It's fun," said the archangel. "Why shouldn't I like it?"

The Little Angel of Generosity rubbed the back of his neck. "No reason. No reason at all."

Tax

Dinah and Jason and Eric got off the school bus together and walked the block and a half home.

Charlene was scrubbing the bathroom floor while Nathaniel was taking a bath. Dinah smiled. She liked how Charlene was smart like that—mixing her housework with child care without Nathaniel even noticing.

"Hi, Charlene. I've got to run an errand. I'll be back soon."

Charlene sat back on her heels. "What kind of errand?"

"Something personal." Dinah hoped her cheeks weren't getting red.

"Oh." Charlene looked curiously at Dinah. "How far are you going?"

"Just as far as the library." That was true— the art store was next door to the library.

"Well, all right. Come back quick. And take one of those cookies your father made to eat on the way."

Dinah put the box of tools in a bag. She grabbed a cookie as she went outside. But she was too nervous to eat it. She put it in her other pocket.

On the bus ride home she had tried to think of what to say—but nothing sounded just right. So there was no point in trying to rehearse. Dinah walked faster. The sooner she got there, the sooner it would be over. She'd give the clerk back the tools.

Only then she wouldn't have a present for Setha.

And she couldn't give Setha the box of clay because Setha was already getting clay from her mother.

Well, Dinah could use the five dollars she'd earned yesterday for something else. Maybe something in the gift store next to the grocery. They had all kinds of stuff.

No, they didn't. They had junk. What Setha really wanted was more art stuff.

Dinah went to open the art store door, but she couldn't. It was as though the door was locked. So she stood outside and stared through the window. All that wonderful stuff. Setha would love almost anything in that store.

The clerk looked up at just that moment and smiled at her.

Dinah turned around and ran home as fast as she could. She put the box of tools on her bed and put the box of clay in the bag instead. Then she stuffed the five-dollar bill in her pocket along with the envelope that still held her change. She counted: three dollars and eighteen cents.

She ran all the way back to the art store.

But the clerk wasn't at the counter.

Dinah walked slowly up to the counter and peeked over, to see if the clerk was maybe kneeling down behind it. No one was there. She looked up and down the aisles. No one. Dinah went back to the counter and now she noticed the little bell that you were supposed to tap to get the clerk's attention. She tapped it.

The clerk came through a door in the back of the store. "Oh, it's you again. I wondered why you ran off."

Dinah handed the clerk the box of clay. "I'm returning this."

"Didn't your friend like it?"

"She already has some." Dinah's head buzzed as if her ears needed to pop. What would happen when she said what she had to say next? She felt faint.

"Well, then, I'll just give you back your money." The clerk went behind the counter.

"No," said Dinah. She held out the five-dollar bill. "I owe you this. And this, too." She handed over the envelope. "I originally had sixteen dollars in the envelope—and that's what's left after I paid for the clay. Plus these five dollars, makes twenty-one dollars. And twenty dollars plus six percent tax makes twenty-one dollars and twenty cents. So I still owe you twenty cents."

"I don't understand."

"It's for the box of tools for cutting clay. The small box."

"Oh, you want to buy a box of tools?"

"No." Dinah looked at the clerk. Then she looked down. "I stole a box. I'm sorry."

The clerk didn't say anything.

Finally Dinah looked up.

The clerk was looking hard at her. "Do you like this store?"

"Yes," whispered Dinah.

"I can't stay open if people steal things." The clerk opened the cash register and put in the money Dinah had given her.

"I'm sorry," whispered Dinah.

"What are you going to do with the tools?"

"I'm giving them to my friend for her birthday. She'll love them," said Dinah. "She's an artist."

72

"That's no reason to have stolen them," said the clerk.

"I know that."

The clerk nodded. "Okay. Bring me the other twenty cents as soon as you can."

"I will." Dinah went to the door.

"One more thing . . . "

Dinah turned to the clerk.

"Promise me you'll never steal again."

"I won't. I've already promised myself." Dinah went out the door and, for the first time in days, she felt genuinely happy. She took Daddy's cookie out of her pocket and munched on it as she walked home.

Angel Thoughts

The newest Archangel of Generosity took one last look through the art store window. He hadn't noticed the bell on the counter before, but when Dinah rang it, he knew he'd earned his wings. What a light, merry sound.

His work here was done. But he had another task waiting—a quick and fun one. He was going to distribute his yo-yo gifts—to his four little angel friends and to the archangel who had guided him. He felt sure all of them would laugh with delight. What could be a better way to celebrate his wings?

Do you want to help?

Every day, the Red Cross helps people in emergencies . . . whether it's half a million disaster victims or one sick child. Their vital work is made possible by people like you, who learn how good it can feel to lend a helping hand. Red Cross "everyday heroes" come from all walks of life. They're all ages. Everyone has something special to offer.

Meet the Little Angel of Fairness in

Angelwings

Not Fair!

Coming soon from Pocket Books!

One for you and one for me, and one for you and one for me." The Little Angel of Fairness counted out chocolate Kisses. Chocolate was her favorite, and Kisses were the best. There was one left over.

"I get it," said the Little Angel of Friendship.

The Little Angel of Fairness pushed her glasses up her nose and neatly arranged her pile of chocolate Kisses into a pyramid. "We have to share it."

"It's too small to share. Plus, if you give it to me, then you'll feel terrific for being generous and I can feel terrific for giving you the opportunity to be so generous."

The Little Angel of Fairness laughed. She unwrapped the tinfoil from the candy Kiss and took out a pair of tiny scissors. "I'll cut it in half, and you can choose the half you want."

"You're going to cut it with scissors?"

"That's all I have. Aren't they cute?" The Little Angel of Fairness cut carefully, but one piece of the Kiss was slightly bigger than the other, anyway.

The Little Angel of Friendship put his hand out toward the big piece. Then he grinned and popped the smaller piece in his mouth.

"Well done," said the Archangel of Fairness. "You're both acting like perfect angels this morning."

"What else would you expect?" said the Little Angel of Friendship.

"Perhaps a bit of humility." The Archangel of Fairness raised her eyebrows in a look of mock scolding. Then she smiled. "Put away your chocolate for now, my little angel, and say good-bye to your buddy." She leaned over the Little Angel of Fairness. "You have a job to do."

"Yay!" The Little Angel of Fairness kissed the other little angel on the cheek. "When I get back, we can play a spinning game with the gold coins I've been collecting."

"But I was supposed to choose our next game," said the Little Angel of Friendship.

"You'll like this game."

"You always choose," said the Little Angel of Friendship. "And I'm always forced to go along."

"So what? You always have fun. My games are the best." The Little Angel of Fairness stuffed her chocolate Kisses into her right pocket. "Oh, I'm so excited. I have all my feathers except for one small patch. This job will fill it in, and I'll earn my wings, I just know I will."

"Good luck," called the Little Angel of Friendship.

The Little Angel of Fairness waved good-bye. Then she took the archangel's hand and held it tightly. "Where are we going?"

"To a driveway in front of a garage."

What kinds of bells are in a garage? wondered the little angel; for every time angels earn their wings, a bell will ring. What kind of bell would ring when she earned her wings?

She put her hand in her left pocket—the one where she kept her gold coins—and she clinked them together softly. They sounded almost like a small, tinkling bell.

Bikes

Hank loosened the nut with a wrench. Then he jiggled his bicycle seat and pulled upward until it was an inch higher. "Just right," he said softly. He opened the pack of spaceship decals he'd bought at the pharmacy and pressed one onto his right handlebar. It shone silvery and perfect.

"Your decals are pretty," said Jessica, coming up behind him. She had a book tucked under one arm. "Will you fix my seat now? It needs to be raised, too. I'm growing as fast as you are."

"You'll never be as tall as me." Hank looked at Jessica's bike, leaning against the side of the garage. "There's a cobweb in your spokes. When's the last time you rode that thing?"

"I forget."

"I'm not going to waste my time working on your bike if you aren't even going to ride it."

"I'll ride it," said Jessica.

"Where?"

"Where are you going to ride yours?" asked Jessica.

"In the high school's Homecoming parade on Saturday afternoon. All my friends are going to be in it."

"I'll ride in the parade, too."

"No way," said Hank. "The bike part of the parade is only for guys."

"That's not fair."

"Come on, Jessica, you can't butt in on a guy thing."

"I can do anything you can."

"Then fix your own seat."

"I'm not strong enough, and you know it." Jessica wrinkled her nose at Hank. "Can I at least have some decals to decorate my bike?"

Hank clutched his decals to his chest. "I

paid for these with my own money."

"I don't have any money," said Jessica.

"So what? I paid, and these decals are mine."

"Remember when you needed sequins for your school project? I let you take a bunch off my dancing costume."

Hank swung one leg over and perched on his bike seat. His feet just reached the ground. "You hated your dancing costume. You hate dancing." He rolled forward. This height for the seat felt good.

"So what?" said Jessica. She took a step and planted herself right in his path. "I shared with you."

"It's not the same thing. Besides, these are spaceships. See?" Hank flashed the decals in front of Jessica's face, then jammed them in his pocket. "They don't go on a girl's bike."

"Oh, yeah? Well, I don't really want them, anyway," said Jessica. "Spaceships have nothing to do with real ships."

"What are you talking about?" asked Hank.

"The theme for Homecoming is always pirates. The high school football team is the Pirates. You know that."

"Of course I know that. But I don't care," said Hank. "Just because the team is the pirates doesn't mean I have to like pirates. But I do like spaceships. And you can't have any of my decals."

"You stink," said Jessica.

"Go read your dumb book," said Hank.

"It's not dumb." Jessica patted her book. "You haven't read it. You never read. I read all the time and I'm a year and a half younger than you. Besides, I just finished my book."

"Then go read another one," said Hank.

"I will. I'll know everything, and you'll know nothing," said Jessica. "And that's how it should be, 'cause you stink."

Don't miss the next

Angelwings

Coming soon from Pocket Books!

The Little Angel of Imagination loves to do creative things, like paint pictures and make up stories. But will it take a lot more than just imagination to help Louie . . .

Louie's little brother always wants to make up silly games, like pretending the family dog is actually a racehorse. But Louie won't play along – he thinks made-up games are for babies. He'd rather watch TV after school than play outside. What's to be done about this lazybones? The Little Angel of Imagination has a plan that might just work.

Angelwings

Donna Jo Napoli knows just how it feels to have a problem that you don't think you can solve by yourself. "All of us have problems, some big and some small. And all of us who solve those problems have help, whether we recognize that help or not. If we keep our hearts open, we can help and be helped more easily. I offer these books as a gift to your open heart."

Donna Jo Napoli's award-winning novels are read all over the world. She is the head of the linguistics department at Swarthmore College in Pennsylvania, where she lives with her husband and their children.